BLUE BUNNY BLACKBERRY KEEPER

BY HEIDI NIELSEN THIESE

First Edition

ISBN: 978-1-7354804-0-4 (paperback)
           978-1-7354804-1-1 (ebook)

Book design by TeaBerryCreative.com

To Mom and Dad and Daniel, for bringing Blue Bunny to life and for teaching me to ask hard questions.

To Aaron, for encouraging me to embrace abundance. Life with you is rich in love.

To Jonah and Greta, for reminding me to do the right thing even when it's hard. You are my joy.

PROLOGUE

Sometimes Blue Bunny felt like he could remember. He felt he had been there at the beginning, in the stillness and quiet, before the earth began. The memory was warm and safe, hidden in the deepest part of his heart, the part he could hear only if he was very quiet.

That is the thing most creatures don't know about bunnies. They are good listeners. It's the ears. A bunny can learn a lot by just listening. By being still. By hearing what others do not.

So, the little bunny, with fur so gray it was almost blue, listened. He listened for the story his heart knew.

Leaning into Grandpa Bunny's side, he whispered through trembling whiskers, "Tell me the story. Tell me the story of the beginning."

"Again?" came a gentle reply.

"Yes, again."

"Alright, my love. Snuggle in. Rest your head."

And Blue Bunny did just that, leaning into Grandpa Bunny's soft, safe fur.

"This is not my story. It is not a bunny story. It is the story of all creatures.

Are you ready?

I will tell you.

Listen."

Blue Bunny exhaled and quieted his heart. The campfire hissed and crackled. Wood smoke curled into his fur. Sparks drifted up to meet the stars.

Each word rolled carefully from Grandpa's rich voice, composing a deliberate, patterned song.

Blue Bunny whispered along to the rhythm, the hymn in his heart.

In the beginning
Before the earth was born
There was nothing

Nothing to see
Nothing to hear
Nothing to feel

Out of nothing
Came everything
Out of darkness, came light
Out of silence, came singing
Out of emptiness, came joy

The creator
Made

Moonlight and tides
Made
Waves and whispering trees
Made
Sun and rain and soil

She made
Us
She made
You

Her breath
Her heart
Outside herself

"Wise Raven looked over all she had made. Her eyes, two ebony mirrors, reflected earth's beautiful mystery. Her heart filled with love. Love dripped from the sky onto the earth, overflowing its rivers, brimming its oceans. Love seeped into the hearts of the creatures, filling them to bursting.

"With each drop, Wise Raven whispered, 'This is love. This is enough. Share it and it will never run out.'"

Blue Bunny's heart beat faster. The story entered him and became part of him. It made its way to the quiet, hidden place in his heart. It lodged itself there, creating a profound longing.

Grandpa Bunny continued, "Wise Raven knew her creatures needed a reminder of her love and abundance.

So she gave us a gift. She gave us a map, with a promise that when we follow it, we will find what we are looking for."

With each word, each pause, each inflection, Blue Bunny knew he belonged to something bigger than he could ever imagine. He imagined himself as part of the story. He braced himself for what he knew was next.

Grandpa's voice grew soft and melancholy. "At first the creatures feasted and danced and laughed and loved. They tended crops. They harvested food. They celebrated enough berries to last through storms and snow.

"But then the creatures forgot. Summer waned. Shadows lengthened. Blackberries withered on the vine. Harvest after harvest passed. And the Creator's whisper of love was traded for a whisper of 'not enough'.

"Fear festered in the creatures' hearts. They stopped celebrating what they had and began to worry about what they did not have. They forgot to hold their arms wide and instead held them close. They forgot to open their hearts to love and they became dry and parched.

"They held on tight. They held tighter. But it wasn't enough. The tighter they held on, the more their fear grew, until they held so tight, they couldn't breathe, couldn't live, couldn't love."

A gentle mist had formed while Grandpa Bunny was telling the story, its droplets mingling with the fire's smoke. Blue Bunny was aware of the trees surrounding them, listening, waiting.

Blue Bunny leaned forward. He held his breath and

turned to look directly into Grandpa Bunny's eyes. "Then what happened?" he whispered, expectant.

Grandpa held him closer. "The ending is not yet written, my Blue Bunny. It is an invitation."

Blue Bunny closed his eyes. Someday, he would like to write that part of the story. He hoped it would be a story filled with abundance instead of fear. He hoped it would be a story that explained the quiet place in his heart, longing for more. For most bunnies, the story of the beginning was just that, a story, worn and predictable from years of telling. But for Blue Bunny, it felt different.

Every time he heard the story, he knew something. He knew the story was real. He knew the story was bright and mysterious, calling him. He knew in deepest part of his heart, the part he could hear only if he was very quiet, that he was created to be part of the story.

CHAPTER 1

WHISPERINGS

Blue Bunny was about to close the atlas, his book of maps, when he thought he heard the slightest whisper. Like the way wind rustles through fir boughs, though part of him was sure he hadn't heard anything. He paused and waited to see if the sound would come again, beckoning him, but all was still and silent.

The cracked spine felt at home in his paw. He had held this same atlas countless times before without a sound. Its maps were covered with tiny markings, notations of secret rocks and ravines. Secret caves and trees. Secret hiding places. Written by generations of bunnies, some markings were faded but still spoke of adventure and mystery. He looked at the fine lines and squiggles that crept across the paper, leading him somewhere.

Curious, he placed his ear flat against the map. The sound came again, louder, and more insistent. The whisper became a murmur, then a siren's song, and finally a crescendo of longing.

Startled, he dropped the worn parchment. Paper didn't talk, did it? And it certainly didn't sing. I will not be afraid, Blue Bunny told himself. I'm imagining things. But his heart knew different.

And he knew he needed to return the ancient atlas to Grandpa Bunny soon. He had again spent his afternoon pouring over its pages. Of all the books he read while he sat in his orchard reading nook, safe against an apple tree, the atlas was his favorite. Reading it, he felt calm and certain.

He held it in his paws, paper crinkling. One page, one map in particular, tucked in the back of the atlas, held an energy, a magic buzzing vibrancy. He placed a paw on the spot marking his orchard home, the very place he was sitting. When he lifted it, he saw a tiny mark, a jagged leaf, encircled by an intricate vine. Blue Bunny stared at it intently. He had never noticed it before. He pulled his notebook and pencil from his vest pocket. He copied the image, careful to capture the leaf's patterned lines, lush paths edged with teeth and surrounded by thorns.

He wondered what it meant.

He heard the whisper, louder this time. Somewhere, on this page, Blue Bunny thought, lies a secret.

Shadows lengthened. Twilight beckoned magic.

He gently folded and closed the giant atlas. He wondered if a book could come alive. He wondered if it could tell him things. He wondered if it could change the course of his path.

CHAPTER 2

ANOTHER STORY

The summer sun cast a golden glow on the orchard. Atlas tucked under his arm, Blue Bunny set off on the well-worn path to Grandpa's workshop. Salmon berries winked orange in their groves. The ripening of these tart jewels would be followed closely by huckleberries, blueberries, and finally, the culmination of summer's harvest, the blackberry.

The wild blackberries, the ones that had grown in small pockets of the forest for as long as the bunnies could remember, were rare and sweet, small, hidden, dark gems. Each summer, after a whole year of waiting, Blue Bunny longed for their taste on his tongue. They tasted like treasure. They tasted like home. They tasted like the beginning.

They tasted like Grandpa Bunny's story felt. Warm, safe, and part of something bigger than himself.

Blue Bunny spotted a group of beavers busily filling baskets with berries, awaiting transformation into jam and pie and scones. Roy the Beaver paused his picking and waved. He tipped his hat and whistled through his teeth, "I'm hoping to pick enough for jam, Blue Bunny. Looks like a small crop this season, yes indeed, but I'm hopeful."

Blue Bunny smiled, knowing Roy's sweet tooth, and hoped too, for enough berries.

Blue Bunny passed trees with the beginnings of tiny apples hanging from spidery branches. Ancient plum trees, dripping with lichen, bowed across the trail. He went deeper into the forest. Even now, in the warmth of the afternoon, there were parts of the forest floor hidden from the sun, obscured by layers of firs and ferns.

The wind breathed through the trees. Shadows swallowed sunlight. Something brushed against his shoulder. Blue Bunny whirled around, expecting to meet a monster but saw only the dancing branches.

A glint of light caught the corner of his eye, the smallest of changes in the forest shadows. A reflection perhaps. A twinkle. For a moment, he thought he saw a defined shape amidst the moss. A flash of fur. A glinting tooth. He paused, searching the layers of green for a distinct form. Stillness met his senses. I must be imagining things, he thought. Heart skittering in his chest, he went on.

Above him, a clawed paw lowered a set of binoculars. A pair of liquid golden eyes gleamed. Their satisfied owner replaced the binoculars with a pair of sunglasses and turned to its accomplice, who hypnotically twitched his tail and pulled up the collar of a sleek brown trench coat. "Follow him," he growled.

Grandpa Bunny's workshop was a place of wonder.

The workbench was covered with all manner of instruments and tools, the remains of past experiments and the beginnings of new ones.

Jars containing soil, seeds, and sprouts, meticulously labeled, lined the walls. Shelves held beakers, glass tubing, and seedlings cradled in old tin cans.

Stacks of botany books reached to the ceiling, where they met an upside-down garden of dried herbs and moss.

Humming happily to himself in the middle of it all was Grandpa Bunny. Upon seeing Blue Bunny, he grinned. He rose from a well-worn stool and straightened his vest, into which he tucked his safety goggles.

Blue Bunny's heart smiled. He loved coming to Grandpa Bunny's workshop. He spent hours exploring while Grandpa Bunny was working, examining each contraption he created. Grandpa always had a project, an idea come to life. Blue Bunny found his clever curiosity contagious. He inquired after each thing, holding it in his paws. Grandpa Bunny answered every question, addressed every curiosity. He reveled in the process.

"I brought you the atlas." Blue Bunny hesitated as he handed it back. Should he mention he heard something odd? Should he mention he thought the atlas was talking to him? It never had before. Would Grandpa Bunny believe him?

Before he could ask, Grandpa Bunny watched the

questions cross his face and motioned for him to settle in.

"Blue Bunny, I need to tell you a story."

"The story of the beginning?" Blue Bunny asked eagerly.

"Not today. A different story. A new story."

A new story! Blue Bunny perched on the stool. He held his breath. He pulled out his notebook and pencil for good measure. He may just need to jot down an idea. The picture of the jagged leaf waited.

Grandpa Bunny began, looking thoughtful. "This is our story. Our family's story. Your story.

"For many years, a bunny in our family has done an important and brave thing. That bunny knows the secret locations of the wild blackberry patches and protects them. That bunny is the Blackberry Keeper."

Blue Bunny listened, trying to understand. This sounded a lot like the story of the beginning, but different. He had heard legends of the Blackberry Keeper, but this story was more specific. More directed at him.

"For many years, I have been Blackberry Keeper. And I have been preparing you to be Blackberry Keeper, keeper of the *Rubus ursinus*, the rare and precious wild blackberry. That is why I have taught you all these years about caring for plants, for cherishing them, for preserving them. It's your turn."

Blue Bunny wrestled with this new idea. He wondered if he could to do an important, brave thing.

"It is time. And you will need this." Grandpa Bunny crossed the worn wood floor and peered into a tiny corner cupboard. He withdrew a small hinged box. Carefully, Grandpa Bunny handed the box to Blue Bunny.

Blue Bunny lifted the lid. Inside was a tiny metal disc, an intricate wreath of gold vines outlining its edge. Grandpa Bunny lifted it lovingly and placed it in Blue Bunny's paw. The smooth, cool metal felt both foreign and familiar. He traced the circumference and felt a tiny indentation along the surface. Curious, he allowed his paw to pause and with a click, the disc opened. Inside, like a hidden star, was a beautiful compass dial. A tiny red needle hovered over an even tinier letter N.

"This compass belonged to a bunny who lived many years ago. That bunny was your great-great grandmother," whispered Grandpa Bunny. "She was a Blackberry Keeper."

Cradling the compass, Blue Bunny turned and watched the needle spin and stop. Grandpa had taught him about compasses and the magnets within, which attract some things and ignored others. The world is a magnet. A compass will always align itself with the pull of true north. Blue Bunny rotated the compass. The needle moved again, steady in its search.

Grandpa Bunny smiled. "This compass, when used with the atlas, will guide you where you need to go. Blue Bunny, it is time for a new adventure. It is your turn to be Blackberry Keeper. It might be dangerous, more dangerous than ever before. Among our forest friends, there are rumors of ominous dealings. Of ones who do not honor the desire to protect the blackberries. There are those who want to take the blackberries only for themselves. There are whisperings of mystery and sabotage. Of silent, sinister forces."

Blue Bunny wondered about the odd feeling he had on the way here. He asked hesitantly, "Do you mean bad guys?

Stealing and scaring everyone? The bears are always the bad guys in the story, right? And sometimes cougars, I suppose. Aren't they bad too?" He shuddered at the thought of the claws and barred teeth he had been taught to fear.

Grandpa Bunny looked at Blue Bunny and said thoughtfully, "In our stories, they are often are the bad guys, yes. Yet, I wonder. Should they be?"

Blue Bunny wasn't sure what Grandpa Bunny meant by this. He thought he knew the answer to his question even while he asked it. Was Grandpa trying to tell him something different?

Grandpa Bunny continued, "Blue Bunny, you will need to be brave. You will need to learn to do the right thing even when it is hard. Even when it is the hardest thing you have ever done.

"You have the atlas. And as I think you know, it is a particularly special atlas," Grandpa said, winking and handing the atlas back to Blue Bunny. "And now you have the compass. And it is a particularly special compass. Hold them close."

Blue Bunny accepted the atlas from Grandpa and held it close to his chest, spine cracked, pages brittle.

"But how will I know? How will I know the right thing? How will I know what questions to ask? Who to ask?"

Grandpa smiled. "I asked those same questions once. You must remember that you are not alone. You are not meant to be alone. You will have help along the way."

Blue Bunny felt the pull of the atlas, from the maps within. He held the compass. It radiated warmth from his paw to his heart. He left Grandpa's workshop, his head and heart full.

He wandered into the fading light, into a cloak of trees telling tales in whispers. He stopped to listen, and the forest stopped to listen with him.

The silence deepened, opening room for questions. What did it mean to be Blackberry Keeper? Why him? Why not some other bunny? Could he do it?

Blue Bunny felt he had had his daily allotment of puzzles. Visions of talking maps and magic compasses swirled through his mind. He imagined himself following their direction, only to have his path obscured by creeping blackberry vines that closed tightly around him.

It all felt too much.

He allowed himself to lie upon the forest floor. Twigs crackled and leaves rustled. Branches grew toward the canopy, arms reaching for sky, dark tips sweeping the stars. Dazed by their brilliance, dazed by his new knowledge and new task, he didn't hear the approaching sound.

Leaves crunched. A branch snapped. Blue Bunny's neck prickled. Startled, he turned quickly and found himself nose to nose with another creature.

Attached to the nose were bouncing whiskers, and above those, a set of twinkling eyes and floppy ears. "Blue Bunny!" exclaimed a brown whirl of fur.

Blue Bunny laughed, relieved at the sight of his friend.

Brown Bunny grinned.

Brown Bunny, whom he had known for so many years. Brown Bunny, who laughed at his jokes, acted out scenes he read in books, and listened to all his big questions.

Their very first meeting had been marked by a baking

mishap, in which one or the other of them had almost caught fur and forest on fire, and the other had helped squelch the flames. Ever since, they knew they were meant to take care of each other.

CHAPTER 3

A PARTNER

"You're the next Blackberry Keeper?" Brown Bunny asked with awe, after his friend had shared Grandpa's unsettling combination of commissioning and warning. The two friends had settled in for tea and blackberry scones. Crumbs tumbled from Brown Bunny's mouth as he continued. "I didn't know there still was a Blackberry Keeper. I thought they all died out, a long time ago."

Blue Bunny nodded a small nod, his scone untouched. He liked the idea of adventure. The imagining of it. The reading about it. But did he want to do it?

He looked at his friend. At his burrow. At the cozy, root entangled ceiling. At shelves overflowing with books of every kind: botany books with lusciously detailed plant illustrations, adventure stories with conquering heroes, and an entire set of green encyclopedias with gold etched spines, promising to answer questions.

The shelves were built into the walls, flanking a tiled fireplace and tucked behind an overstuffed chair. All of it beckoned Blue Bunny to pick a book and settle in. To escape into someone else's adventure.

Brown Bunny looked at his friend's familiar face and knew he was lost in his thoughts. And those thoughts were usually quite interesting.

"What are you thinking about?" he asked.

"I'm thinking about what I'm supposed to do," replied Blue Bunny, walking outside his front door. "Now that I'm the Blackberry Keeper, Grandpa said I must prepare for something dangerous."

"Dangerous?"

"Yes. Dangerous. He said I will need to be brave. I don't think I've ever had to be brave. I'm not sure if I can." Blue Bunny turned to his friend with a worried look.

Each bunny was full of thoughts. Thoughts about what it meant to be brave. Even when you didn't want to be.

"I am good at being brave. I will be brave with you." declared Brown Bunny, suddenly leaping up and slashing a sword fern frond in great crisscrossing arcs. "To be brave, you must have weapons!" he shouted, slaying imaginary villains.

"Ah, I'm not sure," replied a hesitant Blue Bunny. "Warriors use weapons."

"Aren't we warriors? Isn't that what it means to be brave?" asked Brown Bunny, continuing to wield his fern.

Blue Bunny considered. "Warriors fight using physical strength. I think I'm supposed to fight with the strength of my mind. Grandpa Bunny said I must ask questions and solve a mystery. By myself."

"Mmm," Brown Bunny said, lowering his fern, slightly disappointed. He paused, thought, then raised a finger in the air. "A mystery's afoot. We need hats with floppy flaps! Like detectives." Brown Bunny imagined himself wearing a hat with flaps and couldn't quite figure out how his ears would fit. It would be like having four flaps. "No, no, the hat's not quite right. We need capes!" he exclaimed.

"Capes?" Blue Bunny replied, voice rising in confusion. "Superheroes wear capes."

"Aren't we superheroes?" Brown Bunny asked, shoulders stooping.

"Superheroes do good deeds and rescue each other. Also, I think, by themselves."

Brown Bunny contemplated this. "If you are going to solve a mystery, with the possibility of scary bad guys, I am going to help you. I don't think you should be the Blackberry Keeper all by yourself."

Blue Bunny looked at his friend. Maybe he wasn't meant to do something hard alone. He gave Brown Bunny a small smile. Brown Bunny grinned back. "I've always wanted to be a warrior detective superhero! But if we can't have floppy hats and capes, what do we get to wear?"

"Vests. With pockets. Lots of pockets," replied Blue Bunny, rummaging around the depths of his vest and producing his small notebook. "And our scientific notebooks. One must always make observations.

"We are the two Science Sleuths!" exclaimed Blue Bunny, warming to his friend's contagious enthusiasm.

"The Dual Detectives!" exclaimed Brown Bunny.

"Lagomorph Investigators!" quipped Blue Bunny.

Brown Bunny stopped mid hop. "Wait, what's a lag-o-morph?" he asked, sounding out each strange syllable.

"Oh, it's the scientific name for rabbits—for us."

"I don't know if I can remember how to say that one," Brown Bunny considered. "What about...rabbits...bunnies... off to protect and solve the mystery of the blackberries. I've got it! We're the Bunny Blackberry Brigade!"

"Yes, the Bunny Blackberry Brigade, Blackberry Keepers."

"We work together like the moon and the tide. Like the rain and the clouds. Like the soil and the trees!

We are inseparable.

We are a team.

We are friends."

The two friends hopped back to Blue Bunny's burrow and celebrated their newly named partnership with toast and blackberry jam. Brown Bunny lifted his plate, licked the last of the crumbs, and grinned. Blue Bunny smiled at him. There was always something to be happy about, and Brown Bunny seemed to always find that something.

CHAPTER 4

A VEHICLE
FOR ADVENTURE

Blue Bunny hopped closer to the beast. He peeked between the grass blades, hoping for a closer look. Enormous clear round eyes stared back. A gleaming grill of silver teeth grinned. Two mirrors protruded like ears from either side.

Four black tires encircled smooth surfaced chrome discs. In them, Blue Bunny saw his reflection, his ears stretched to a hilarious length. He giggled.

So often he had admired the enormous, luminous green metal of Grandpa's truck.

A peek in the windows revealed a great steering wheel. A steering wheel! Oh, the possibilities.

"It appears to be unattended," came a voice behind him.

Startled, Blue Bunny turned. "Unattended?"

"Precisely. I suggest you liberate it," beamed Grandpa Bunny.

"Liberate it?" echoed Blue Bunny in a smaller voice.

"Yes, let it be free. Uninhibited. This vehicle needs

appreciation. Adventure. And the new Blackberry Keeper is certainly in for some adventure."

Blue Bunny looked at Grandpa inquiringly. "Are you suggesting I drive it?"

Grandpa Bunny's eyes twinkled. "Indeed I am."

"But where do I go? How do I start?" worried Blue Bunny.

Grandpa Bunny smiled warmly. "Study the map. Trust the compass. Listen. And you will know where to go."

Before Blue Bunny could utter another protest, Brown Bunny suddenly appeared, eyes bright with excited anticipation. "Let's go! Hop in."

"I'll get my vest," conceded Blue Bunny.

It is a truth universally acknowledged that a bunny in possession of a map, a compass, and a vehicle must be in want of an adventure. Blue Bunny was still learning this truth, certainly, as his lifelong best friend and newly minted partner, coaxed him to the driver's seat. Admiring a vehicle and actually driving it are two very different things.

"You drive. I'll shift. Ten and two!" announced Brown Bunny, closing the door and hopping to the passenger side.

"Ten and what?" inquired a perplexed Blue Bunny, studying an array of buttons and levers decorating the dashboard. "Do you mean twelve?"

"No, on the steering wheel. Pretend it's a giant clock. One paw at the two o'clock position. The other paw at the

10 o'clock position. I read it in a book once—*Worst Case Scenario: How to Drive a Car Without Opposable Thumbs.*"

Eyebrows raised, Blue Bunny cautiously placed his front paws where he imagined numbers on the clock face steering wheel. "Now what do I do?" he asked, perched in the driver's seat, back paws dangling.

Brown Bunny considered. "I suppose if you want to reach the pedals, you'll have to steer with your ears. Like this." Brown Bunny demonstrated a sitting position that could only be attributed to a wayward circus act—his two tiny bunny hind paws scrambling between three floor pedals and his silky ears wrapped around the steering wheel. "Now, you try," he eagerly suggested, scooting across the great vinyl bench seat to the passenger side.

Blue Bunny hesitatingly recreated his friend's contortion—paws on the pedals, ears on the wheel. "But I can't see," he worried.

"Oh, that's all right. I'll see for you. Trust me."

With that pronouncement, Brown Bunny produced a key from under the floor mat and turned the ignition. The engine roared to life.

Blue Bunny reluctantly released the clutch. The green metal monster lurched through the orchard and into the forest, past startled chipmunks and chickadees. It lunged around the corner of the driveway, seeking freedom of the open road. From the trees, deer watched, wide eyed.

Ears furiously spinning, Blue Bunny cranked the steering wheel and haphazardly pulled onto the pavement, leaving behind the safety of the forest. "Which way?" he yelped, eyeballs level with the wheel, blurry green trees whizzing by in his periphery.

"Turn left!" yelled Brown Bunny, who was simultaneously clutching the atlas, gripping the seat for dear life, and grinning ear to ear.

Blue Bunny spun the wheel, sliding Brown Bunny the length of the vinyl bench seat and into the passenger door handle.

"Turn right!" came the next direction, which resulted in Brown Bunny flying the opposite way and crashing into his friend.

"Why aren't you wearing your seatbelt?" cried Blue Bunny.

"Oh, that must be what this is for," Brown Bunny answered, lifting a gray strap attached to a giant metal buckle and clicking it satisfactorily in place. Now able to concentrate more fully on navigation and less on staying put, Brown Bunny happily riffled through the atlas' pages. Blue Bunny peeked at the compass in his vest pocket, trusting its magic. The needle spun, first wildly, then with certainty, directing them to the tiny letter W. "I think we need to go west. Good adventures always seem to start in the west."

CHAPTER 5

A Mystery and a Clue

Driving proved easier with practice and Blue Bunny slowly relaxed to the point he was enjoying himself.

He accelerated. Evergreens blurred outside the window.

Blue Bunny was happy. He was a bunny riding with his best friend on a summer's day, ready for an adventure. He wriggled his nose out the window and breathed in earth and moss tinged with the sweet tang of berries.

His heart was full.

His tummy, however, was not full. "I'm feeling a bit hungry," he declared.

"Let's see what sort of provisions we have here," said Brown Bunny, voice echoing in the cavernous glove box.

"Banana?" he offered, extracting the yellow fruit from its depths.

Blue Bunny wrinkled his nose in distaste.

"Okay then," Brown Bunny continued, disappearing

onto the floorboards. After further rummaging, his raised a triumphant paw. "Bran muffin?"

Blue Bunny raised an eyebrow. "Where did you find that?"

"Under the seat," Brown Bunny proudly exclaimed.

Blue Bunny considered their culinary options. "Blackberry Keepers need good thinking food. Something to savor. Something sweet."

"Mmm," agreed Brown Bunny. "Something comforting."

"Blackberry pie!" they said in unison, quite pleased that their first decision as an official team involved delicious decadence.

"To the Rhododendron Café!" Blue Bunny proclaimed, flexing his ears and turning the wheel toward the winding country road that led to his favorite restaurant. The road skirted a lush valley of farms, deep green fields dotted with grayed cedar barns. Foothills rolled beyond, crowned by majestic mountains, reflecting the golden sun.

They pulled into the café's parking lot, tires crunching on the gravel. The metal monolith of the truck blended in with the tractors and trailers, distributing and collecting loads of hay and grain from the neighboring feed and seed. Blue Bunny parked, quickly tucking the atlas into his vest pocket before jumping from the truck.

In their excitement, neither bunny noticed the flash of fur, the glint of a tooth behind the truck.

A neon sign, welcoming the bunnies to the Rhododendron Café, flickered pink. Over the sounds of clinking coffee pots, Blue Bunny could hear singing. It drifted from the kitchen, way off key.

Blue Bunny smiled, pushed open the swinging door, and landed on a sticky swivel stool, all in one swift hop.

A perky squirrel, bedecked in bracelets and babbles, joyfully squeaked at the sight of him. "Blue Bunny! And Brown Bunny! How wonderful!"

She clapped her paws and giggled, sending her sleek brown tail, covered in purple ribbons, bouncing. Her apron pockets brimmed with straws and pens and utensils, nestled away for future use. Above this overflow were layers of glittering necklaces and a sequined nametag, which read "Margaret".

Margaret flitted back and forth behind the front counter, grabbed her pencil and order pad and warmly asked, "Out for an adventure today? What would you like to eat?"

Brown Bunny eyed the pasty case, momentarily forgetting about pie. Bear claws gushed apple filling. Banana Slug bars oozed custard. Marmot maple bars dripped frosting.

Brown Bunny imagined himself taking a big, delicious bite. Closing his eyes, he tried to imagine which one he wanted most. A question interrupted his daydream.

"Do you have any wild blackberry pie today?" Blue Bunny asked eagerly. "We know yours is the best around."

"Ah, it is delicious, my loves," she smiled with a hint of melancholy. "It is delicious indeed, but it is gone. It's been gone for days."

"Gone? What do you mean gone?" asked a perplexed Blue Bunny.

She leaned toward the bunnies, eyes quickly scanning the restaurant and whispered, "Who sent you?"

"Sent us?" asked Brown Bunny, clearly a little too loudly for the fidgety squirrel.

Margaret glanced nervously around, her bright eyes shifting from left to right, from right to left, as if expecting to find something, or someone, lurking in the shadows. She lowered her voice further. "There have been inquiries."

Blue Bunny and Brown Bunny looked at each other with confusion. "Inquiries?"

Margaret hesitated, eventually discerning her long-time friends could be trusted. "Questions about forest secrets. Treasure. And a magic map." Blue Bunny's heart skipped a beat thinking about the contents of his vest pocket.

"And disappearances."

Brown Bunny gasped, "Disappearances?"

Margaret held a finger to her lips. "Disappearances. Vanishings. Someone is here and then, poof, they're gone."

"Poof?" echoed Blue Bunny.

"It's always the same," she whispered, leaning in. "Someone comes in looking for berries. Blackberries. The rare ones—wild blackberries. In anything—pie, cobbler, jam, milkshakes. And anyone who knows anything about them, where to pick them, how to bake them, vanishes. They simply disappear.

"Myrtle, our head pie baker, usually arrives at the café first thing in the morning. She starts baking, rolling pie crusts, heaping them with berries, and slipping them in the oven. Their scent wafts outside, drifts down the road, and greets our first customers."

Brown Bunny licked his lips with a dreamy look in his eye.

Margaret continued, "But one morning, I didn't smell the sweet scent. I didn't hear her humming. I didn't feel the warmth of the oven. I opened the door, and everything was dark."

Margaret's bracelets jangled. She leaned in and whispered, "It appears Myrtle woke up one morning, headed to work, and never made it."

A chill traveled down Blue Bunny's spine and settled in his chest. He longed to do what he did whenever his heart felt restless. He had an intense sudden need to hold and look at the atlas. So often, when things felt uncertain or scary, the maps inside helped him feel better. He slipped his paw inside his pocket and opened the atlas.

While he had looked at it so many times, something new stood out. At the edge of the page, at the location of the café, was a new marking, a tiny flower. Blue Bunny studied its delicate petals, like a five pointed star, nestled against a lush leaf with jagged edges, encircled by an intricate vine. He stopped.

There was something familiar about this leaf and vine. He lifted the map and held it into the light. It looked out of place and familiar at the same time. Where had he seen that shape before?

Blue Bunny pulled his notebook from his pocket and looked at his last few entries. He quietly compared his sketch, copied from the map in the orchard, to the mysterious new picture. The leaf and vine were identical. Quickly, he sketched the new mark, with the flower, wondering what it could mean.

Brown Bunny, meanwhile, seemed hardly able to contain his astonishment and outrage. "Myrtle. Missing? It can't be!" He turned to his friend, pleading, "Blue Bunny, we have to find her. This is a perfect first case for us! Bunny Blackberry Brigade, Blackberry Keepers at your service!" he announced to Margaret, snapping to mock attention.

Blue Bunny hesitated. The part of his heart he could hear in the quiet seemed far away. Was this part of being the Blackberry Keeper? "I don't know. I'm not sure we could help."

Margaret seemed unaware of his hesitation. "You know who you should talk to," she chirped, ribbons bouncing, "That old goat who runs the co-op store. He knows more than he lets on—may have some idea about what's happening."

Blue Bunny raised a quizzical eyebrow. In his experience, goats didn't tend to be reliable sources of information. He supposed it was the seemingly constant distraction of food. He found it quite difficult to listen to someone talk through a munching mouth.

Brown Bunny seemed less concerned. "Let's give it a try. What do we have to lose?"

CHAPTER 6

ANOTHER MARK

Back in the truck, as he tucked the atlas in the glove box for safekeeping, Blue Bunny felt less certain about his desire for adventure. Or danger. Or his ability to help anyone. How had taking care of blackberries turned into a search for a missing animal and the very likely dangerous criminal who kidnapped her?

He was thinking these gloomy thoughts when rain began to splatter on the windshield. Clouds loomed above.

Blue Bunny gripped the steering wheel. The truck's tires slipped on the newly slick pavement. The truck spun and swirled and flew right off the road, into a wide, wet ditch. The glove box flew open. The atlas and banana and bran muffin flew through the air, landing against the windshield with a thump.

Blue Bunny let out a great breath. This was more complicated than he imagined. The atlas slid across the dashboard, spilling maps. How could he possibly solve a mystery, save his friends, and save the blackberries?

How does someone simply vanish? One moment, you know where they are. The next you don't. He recalled the conversation with Margaret. "Poof," she had said. Well, it must be more than "poof". Things just don't happen without an explanation.

Brown Bunny interrupted his morose thoughts, talking from behind one of the maps splayed across the dashboard.

"What is that?" Brown Bunny asked, pointing to a tiny mark on the map.

Blue Bunny peered at the mark, a plump dark berry resting against a jagged leaf, encircled by an intricate vine. The same leaf and vine he had just seen in the café. Only now in a different place on the map. "It's a new mark!" he whispered. Blue Bunny paused. He looked at Brown Bunny's confused expression. And he decided to trust his friend. "I think the map is trying to tell me something," he said haltingly, ready for Brown Bunny to laugh. But he didn't.

Blue Bunny shared more. "I think the map is trying to lead us somewhere. This mark, the one you see, is like one I saw the day the map first talked to me, in the orchard. The day I became Blackberry Keeper. That day, I saw a leaf. And I saw another mark while we were sitting in the café, a flower. And now it's become a berry and is somewhere else. Here," he said, pointing to the tiny spot on the map, "on this mountain. And I think it's connected to something bigger!"

He pulled out his notebook and showed Brown Bunny the drawing he made in the orchard and the drawing to he made in the café. Slowly, he lifted his notebook next to the map, comparing the marks.

Brown Bunny stared at his friend, mouth open.

The pull of the map felt stronger than ever. Beckoning him somewhere. Toward a secret.

"Let's go find a goat," Brown Bunny declared.

Blue Bunny nodded. "Help me pull us out of this ditch."

He hopped from the truck and tied a winch cable to a nearby tree. Slowly, the truck, pulled by its own engine, emerged from the muck. Brown Bunny watched the wheels spatter mud high into tangled branches. He saw something more than dirt and tree. Perched above its prey, a mouth of razor-sharp teeth grinned. A pair of sunglasses winked. A trench coat flapped in the wind.

"Get in the truck!" yelped Brown Bunny.

CHAPTER 7

ANOTHER MAP

High atop a great cliff perched the animal co-op store, keeping watch over the seaside town. No coming or going—be it by paw, water, or sky—escaped its benevolent eye. Blue Bunny tilted his head back, searching for its top. His gaze was met by fluffy clouds skirting across its spire.

Rickety stairs led haphazardly to a narrow doorway. Brown Bunny pushed open the door. A bell tinkled high above, signaling their entrance. Light streamed through high arched windows, catching bits of dust in its rays. The air smelled of spices and wood oil. Blue Bunny saw a derelict collection of seashells and what looked to be an entire whale skeleton, suspended from the ceiling. An untidy jumble of flour bins, pickle barrels, and berry baskets covered every inch of floor. The walls were hung with great stretches of fish netting, filled with bits of line and glass floats. A briny breeze let itself in, brushing the objects together like wind chimes.

It was a peculiar assortment, made all the more peculiar by its proprietor.

A contented munching noise met Blue Bunny's ears. Right upon the countertop, stood a goat in a black turtleneck, a black beret, and large horn-rimmed glasses, placidly eating a stack of important looking papers.

"Ah, hello, Mr. Goat? Mr. Beat Nick?" called Blue Bunny.

"Hey cool cats," the goat greeted with a deep voice punctuated by munching sounds.

"Bunnies, we're bunnies," Blue Bunny corrected. Beat didn't seem to notice. He kept right on chewing. "What can I do for you?"

"Well, um, we have a mystery to solve. And we're looking for clues. Margaret at the Rhododendron Café thought you may be able to help."

"Cool. Margaret sure does serve a good pie. Blackberry is my favorite. Wild mountain blackberry pie. I'd do anything for one of those." Beat licked his lips with a faraway look in his eye.

Brown Bunny glanced sideways at Blue Bunny. "Margaret says there may not be any blackberry pie this season." He leaned in, lowering his voice. "She said that the pie makers are going missing!"

Beat seemed unphased by this news. "You don't say?" he considered, calmly stroking his goatee. "I don't know anything about anyone going missing, but I sure know a good place to hide."

"Hide?"

"Sure, folks who are missing don't just vanish. They go somewhere."

Blue Bunny took out his notebook like a real detective.

He smoothed a fresh page, pencil poised.

"Whoa, that's one ace set up," noted Beat, longingly sniffing its pages. Blue Bunny hugged it closer. Beat seemed to have a particular fondness for paper.

"For the kidnapers or the kidnaped?" Blue Bunny redirected.

"For who and what's that now?" Beat looked confused.

"The place to hide. You mentioned you know a good place?" Blue Bunny prompted, becoming increasingly concerned with the reliability of Beat's information.

"Oh, right. Don't know. Could be a place to hide. Could be a place to be hidden. You dig me?"

"We have to dig a tunnel?" asked an even more confused Blue Bunny. Bunnies and even bunny Blackberry Keepers were good at a lot of things, but excavation was not one of them.

"No digging needed. The tunnels are already there. Have been for over a hundred years. Moles built 'em."

"Moles?" echoed Blue Bunny, pencil hovering.

"Moles. Never quite sure what they're up to. Built a huge fort on the cliffs, all connected underground. They don't use them anymore. All that work for nothing. It's the bears that use them now. I'd be careful if I were you. They're up to no good, it you ask me. Usually are, bears. Except the big one. The big one's okay."

"The big one?" gulped Blue Bunny.

"Just go with it."

"Go with what?" Blue Bunny asked, exasperated, uncertain trusting his life to "just go with it" when faced with glib bears, who presumably had big mouths and teeth, was wise.

"With everything," Beat called over his should, as he sauntered toward the back of the store. "Catch you later cool cats."

"Bunnies, we're bunnies," Blue Bunny muttered under his breath.

CHAPTER 8

Into the Dark

Despite his obtuse manner, Beat Nick had provided a map to the fort. After setting down his pencil, he had gazed at the paper longingly, at which time Blue Bunny grasped it quickly in order it avoid its consumption.

The map was a mass of squiggles and hastily drawn landmarks. The map's end point, the fort entrance, was marked with a skull and cross bones. It was not reassuring. It looked like the type of place where a bunny, or two bunnies, could very easily get lost.

Outside the co-op, shadows had lengthened. Blue Bunny opened the truck's heavy door. He wanted to compare Beat's map to the road atlas.

He reached for the glove box, anticipating the feel of the worn, large atlas in his paws. But instead of reassuring paper, his paw met empty space. He gasped. The atlas. It was missing! But he couldn't have lost it. He was certain he had locked it into the glove box. He searched the seat and the floorboards without luck. As he clambered into the backseat, a glint of glass caught his eye. The back window was broken. Smashed, he realized, as he saw a brick on the floor. And then a sickening thought occurred to him. He wasn't the only one who wanted to read the atlas. It had been stolen.

The bunnies climbed into the truck and once again, embarked on their adventure. This time, the thrill of driving was lost amidst his worries over the missing atlas. The missing animals. Fear swirled inside his chest as they followed Beat's map.

The road away from the co-op wound past steep sea cliffs overlooking a watery crossroads. In one direction, lay intricate inlets and bays, the other, vast ocean. A small lighthouse held steady above the waves. Gulls cried out, if in glee or in warning, Blue Bunny was not certain.

The fort's dark entrance gaped like a mouth, its windows empty eyes. It was darker and larger than Blue Bunny had imagined it to be.

His whiskers trembled. He hesitated. Grandpa Bunny said this may be hard. Dangerous. Hearing stories about heroes and villains and adventures was quite different than actually being in those stories. He was no hero, he thought. He was just a bunny with funny looking fur.

Brown Bunny came to stand behind his friend.

"Just go with it," he grinned, handing Blue Bunny a backpack, opening its zipper to reveal a plethora of supplies. Inside, bandages and matches and twine jumbled together. Blue Bunny thought he spotted a hatchet.

"Where did you find this?" Blue Bunny asked.

"In the glove box!" Brown Bunny beamed, donning a head lamp. "I found it when we were searching for the atlas." Blue Bunny was beginning to think that glove box was bottomless. But even with a complete set of supplies, his certainty waivered. He glanced at the fort entrance and shivered. "It seems quite creepy."

"Don't worry," assured Brown Bunny. "There are two of us. Two bunnies are twice as brave as one bunny. Are you ready?"

Blue Bunny hesitated. He wasn't quite certain what he should be ready for. Certain death in a creepy dark passage? The answer to life's mysteries? The reason why he was the Blackberry Keeper?

He remembered all the missing animals. Now was the time. He took a deep breath, hugged his compass to his chest, and stepped into the darkness.

The halo of the headlamp offered a small reassurance, even as the glow bounced eerily off the concrete walls. The ceiling disappeared into darkness. The corridor was dark and dank, full of wet dripping noises. It looked as though no one had been inside for a very long time. Except, maybe, a creature with liquid golden eyes and razor-sharp teeth. Blue Bunny spotted the unmistakable track of a cougar. An exceptionally large cougar. He crouched down and peered at the imprint of toes and claws. It spread wide across, wide enough for several bunny paws to fit inside.

The sound of slamming metal echoed in the cavernous room. A rusted door howled on its hinges.

"What was that?" Blue Bunny asked nervously, whipping

around, ears cocked. They were met only with the slow dripping of dank water. For a moment he thought he saw a small movement. Perhaps a small shy mouse? A scuttering spider?

"Hello?" he called, his voice echoing along the concrete walls. But he was only met by headlamp's shifting light, reflecting off the glistening floor. Blue Bunny reached out, his heart thudding. His fur brushed against something wet and slimy. A startled slug shrank into shadow.

Blue Bunny swallowed. He took a small step forward, singing softly.

"I love to go a-wandering
Along the mountain track"
His words echoed back to him in song.
"Val-deri, val-dera,
Val-deri, val-dera,
Ha, ha, ha, ha, ha, ha."
He stepped gingerly over a puddle, his singing more robust.
"Val-deri, val-dera
Val-deri, val-dera..."
This time it was not his own voice he heard back.
"Heh, heh, heh," a sinister voice joined his chorus.
Blue Bunny froze.

The forced laugh emanated from a chamber, hidden to the right of the corridor. "What do we have here?" Two figures appeared, their shadows grotesquely magnified on the dank wall. The larger, bulkier of the two wore a long brown trench coat, belted at the waist. The smaller, wiry one, wore sunglasses. Blue Bunny scarcely had time to recognize their impracticality in the dark as his heart raced with fear.

"Well, well, well. Two little bunnies," purred the larger cougar. "You wouldn't know anything about a Blackberry Keeper bunny, would you? Know who he is? We hear there's a pretty price to be paid for the Blackberry Keeper. He's supposed to have a magic compass.

"Tell you what, we'll make you a deal. If you tell us where we can find that compass, we'll let you go. No harm done."

The compass seemed to nestle deeper into his vest pocket, willing itself secret. Blue Bunny recognized its importance now that the atlas was missing. Whoever had the atlas had only part of what they needed to find the blackberries. They would need the compass to read it. Blue Bunny was sure the cougars could hear the compass, feel it, resting against his chest, singing with his heartbeat, just as he did.

He would not let them know he had the compass. He would not give away his secret.

CHAPTER 9

THE GREAT JAM ESCAPE

"A magic compass? What can you use it for?" Blue Bunny asked innocently, slowly edging a single paw toward the lighted end of the tunnel.

"You don't need to worry about that, little bunny," the sunglass wearing cougar laughed, oblivious to Blue Bunny's silent movement. "You just help me get that compass into the right paws and you'll be rewarded."

Blue Bunny shrank back from the cougar's hot breath. Pressed against the wet wall, he inched a second paw toward escape. Mud squished between his toes. He lifted his paw once more, breaking free from the muck. It emitted a small squelch. He froze, peering at the cougar, who appeared unaware of his efforts. He wondered how far he could get before the cougar noticed his not so silent sliding.

He counted to five, ignoring the cougar's incessant inquiries. Slowly, infinitesimally, another paw scooched to freedom. This time he splashed a puddle, finally catching the cougar's attention. "Ah, think you can sneak away, do you?" boomed the cougar, lunging forward.

Suddenly, Brown Bunny twisted away, reached into the backpack, and pulled out a small white plastic packet. In one swift motion, he peeled off the top cover. A sweet, sticky aroma filled the space. Brown Bunny lifted the crinkly plastic aloft and waved it under the cougars' noses. They stopped, entranced, eyes glazed.

"Mmmm, jam," the cougar with sunglasses said dreamily. He licked his lips, reaching toward the tiny packet, hypnotized by its contents. Brown Bunny produced more and more packets from his pockets, ripping off their shiny covers and flinging their contents every which way. As the jam increased, so did the cougars' paralysis. Transfixed, they watched Brown Bunny fling each gelatinous glob.

Finally, the big trenchcoated cougar shook his head, breaking the sugary spell.

"Wait, we don't eat jam. Or berries. We're carnivores."

He smashed the packet to the ground. Free from his jam trance and suddenly angry, his lips curled around gleaming teeth.

"Run!" yelled Brown Bunny.

The two friends scrambled along the corridor, retracing their steps to the light.

The cougars, usually agile, crashed into one another in their haste to grab the bunnies. Their slowed pursuit allowed Brown Bunny time to hurl yet more open packets in their direction. Jam oozed on the walls and dripped from the ceiling.

"Where did you get those? What are they?" asked Blue

Bunny, twisting away from cougar claws and clamoring toward the exit.

"Jam packets! I grabbed them from the table at the Rhododendron Café. Never know when you may need something to slather on a toast snack. Or use as an emergency escape tactic. Although it does seem a shame to waste perfectly good preserved fruit. I picked them up, just in case. Stashed them in the glove box for safe keeping."

"The glove box? Again?" Blue Bunny asked, eyebrows high and even more thankful for his friend's spontaneous hording. Because as he glanced behind him, he saw the cougars' progress had slowed.

Mixed with the muck from the corridor floor, the jam congealed into a sticky mess. The cougars sank into its quicksand like grip, growling at their escaping prisoners.

The last thing Blue Bunny saw as he burst into the light was the lanky sunglass wearing cougar shrugging his shoulders, settling into jam muck, and licking his paws.

CHAPTER 10

HOME AGAIN

While the bunny friends had been traveling the fort depths, eluding evil cougars, the sun had escaped the clouds. The beach beckoned, waves glittering.

Brown Bunny lay on the rarely warm sand. Relieved, Blue Bunny collapsed beside him.

In the distance, a snow peaked triangle rose above its mountain neighbors. Busy otters gathered lunch in kelp beds.

Together, the friends looked out over the waves. "Well, we didn't find a bear," remarked Brown Bunny. "Or the missing animals. Or any blackberries. We did find two quirky cougars who really want a compass."

Blue Bunny laughed. He reached deep into his vest pocket, revealing the shiny round instrument. It winked in the sunlight, a conspirator in their mission.

Brown Bunny gasped. "You had it the whole time?"

Blue Bunny nodded thoughtfully, tilting the compass in the sun's rays. "Grandpa gave it to me when he told me I'm the Blackberry Keeper."

Brown Bunny considered this. "I've been thinking. Why would a cougar want blackberries in the first place? Like they said, they're carnivores. What can cougars do with buckets and buckets of blackberries? They can't possible eat them all."

"Brown Bunny, I think it is time we asked ourselves what we know, what we think we know, and what we don't know." Blue Bunny opened his notebook and settled in to review the facts.

"One. Animals are missing.

Two. The animals who are missing are those who know something about blackberries.

Three. My family are the Blackberry Keepers. Correction. I am the Blackberry Keeper . I'm supposed to know the location of the wild blackberry patches and I protect them."

As he said this, a tickling sensation happened in Blue Bunny's brain. He grasped for something that was ruminating in the back of his mind. Slowly, clarity stuck. The marks from the map. He had only started to see them once he became the Blackberry Keeper. They marked the locations of the wild blackberry patches! And he wasn't the only one who wanted to know where they were.

Blue Bunny was beginning to feel as though he may not be quite safe.

He was beginning to feel that his friends may not be quite safe.

"We have to get the atlas back," he said, with sudden urgency. "The same creatures that have the missing animals have the map. I'm sure of it. Probably in some secret hideout somewhere. If we find the map, we find them. And we must not let them have the compass. The compass is required to read the map. It's the last piece they need to find all the blackberries. We can't let that happen. And we need to talk to Grandpa Bunny."

Blue Bunny had sat in this same spot mere days before, in Grandpa's workshop, ready to ask Grandpa Bunny if maps could talk. Now he was sitting there ready to tell Grandpa the atlas was missing. Things had gone from bad to worse. But Grandpa Bunny knew everything there was to know about maps. And Blue Bunny thought maybe Grandpa believed he could do something hard even when he didn't believe it for himself. He sighed and absent-mindedly slathered blackberry jam onto a scone. He took a deep breath. "Grandpa, can I ask you a question?"

"Of course," replied Grandpa Bunny, turning to him, eyes smiling, "I love questions."

Blue Bunny nodded, considering. There were so many questions he wanted to ask. Where should he begin? What would happen if the atlas was lost forever? Why was he the Blackberry Keeper? What if he couldn't do it? Was he in danger? Were his friends in danger?

He wasn't quite ready to admit he no longer had the atlas. He knew that whoever had the atlas had it hidden somewhere secret. And he had to find that somewhere.

He decided to start at the beginning.

"How do you find a secret hideout?"

Grandpa Bunny looked into Blue Bunny's eyes, considering. "I will ask you a question in return. What do we do, Blue Bunny, when we are lost?"

Blue Bunny hesitated. He hadn't expected to be the one answering questions. He tried to remember all the things Grandpa had taught him. "We orient our compass. We find north. We read the map. We follow directions." Tears pricked in his eyes as he recited what he knew. They threatened to leak out, spilling and soaking his fur. He took a deep breath. "But Grandpa, I lost the map. It's gone. It vanished just like the animals vanished. And I don't know what to do." The words poured out in a rush. Blue Bunny hadn't expected them to come with such force. And he hadn't expected to feel just a tiny bit better after saying them out loud. He worried what Grandpa would say. He must be upset. The atlas was so important. It was the key to it all, and he hadn't done a good job taking care of it.

Grandpa Bunny's voice was steady and kind. "Yes, Blue Bunny, I know the map is missing. And I also know there is more than one kind of map. You hold one kind in your paw. You hold another kind in your heart.

"You know how to listen to the map, Blue Bunny. But you also know how to listen to your heart. And that is a far greater skill." Grandpa looked at him tenderly. "When you listen to your heart, you can find your way even without the map."

Grandpa held out his paw, "Remember the longing feeling you have when you listen to the story?"

Blue Bunny's eyes flew to Grandpa's. How did he know? How did Grandpa know about the place hidden in the deepest part of his heart, the part he could hear only if he was very quiet?

"Remember the invitation of the story?" Grandpa asked. "Each of us must decide who we are in the world. We must decide if we are going to do something hard. Or scary. Or uncertain. Ask yourself who you are and what you want to be. Ask yourself who you are when you've lost your way."

Blue Bunny felt this was an awful lot of decisions. His heart felt heavy with the weighing of them.

Grandpa opened his arms.

In his hug, Blue Bunny felt like Grandpa not only understood him, but believed in him. A new kind of certainly captured Blue Bunny's heart. His purpose clear, he felt something he had not felt in a long time. He felt hope.

Brown Bunny skidded to a halt outside the workshop. "Margaret! Margaret is missing!"

"Missing?" Blue Bunny gasped, woken from his thinking.

"She went poof too!" cried Brown Bunny. "And we have to find her."

Blue Bunny did not consider himself brave. He wasn't like the heroes he read about in his books. He had never rescued anyone, never defeated a villain, never traveled to distant lands.

At this point, Blue Bunny could have walked away. He

could have stayed right there in the orchard, with his cozy burrow, his books, and his blackberries.

But he did not. Because while he still did not consider himself brave, he was curious. Very curious.

Curiosity was what made Blue Bunny a good detective. Curiosity was what made Blue Bunny read the entire set of encyclopedias, titles etched in gold. Curiosity was what made him climb into the driver's seat of a giant green truck. Curiosity was what made Blue Bunny brave enough to venture down a dark, gloomy passageway with no sign of rescue.

He was the Blackberry Keeper for a reason. And the Blackberry Keeper had a plan.

He remembered something. He remembered the tiny marking in the atlas. The dark blackberry and jagged leaf, encircled by an intricate vine.

"Brown Bunny, I have a hunch."

"A hunch?"

"A feeling. An idea. A direction."

He pulled his notebook from his pocket and studied his drawing. He wanted to know what was on the mountain marked by the blackberry.

CHAPTER 11

SUMMIT

The truck hugged the edge of the mountain, winding high into alpine meadows. Trees grew short and sparse. Those which had not survived years of unrelenting ice and wind stood stark and white. Sharp rocks and dry dirt replaced the soft moss and lush ferns of woodlands below. It was as if the mountain had risen from the sea, strained to the sky, and shaken off the forest.

Blue Bunny felt a familiar thumping in his heart. The quiet place inside filled with memory and longing sang in rhythm with his surroundings.

"I love to go a-wandering

Along the mountain track

Val-deri, val-dera,

Val-deri, val-dera,

Ha, ha, ha, ha, ha, ha."

"Um, perhaps we shouldn't sing that song right now. It seemed to summon scary bad guy cougars the last time," said Brown Bunny.

"Oh, good point." Blue Bunny replied. He thought for a moment and switched tunes.

"Yodel eh he hoo.

Yodel eh he hoo!"

"You know how to yodel?" inquired a surprised Brown Bunny.

"Oh, yes, yodeling is a mountain requirement!" he laughed, as they approached a large brown lodge, overlooking cragged peaks.

A crowd had gathered outside. Cameras flashed. Little ones clamored to join the excitement. Curious, Blue Bunny came closer. Hopping to see above the fray, he glimpsed the top of a tan hat, jauntily perched on the head of an enormous bear. Motionless, the bear's presence overshadowed the entrance. Its thick, brown fur was partially covered by an enormous pair of blue jeans, topped by a large gold belt buckle attempting to contain the bear's generous middle.

Blue Bunny studied the iconic figure. He thought he detected the tinniest movement. He looked the bear straight in the eye and drew back, startled.

"Did that bear statue just wink at you?" asked Brown Bunny.

"I think it did." Blue Bunny looked around. Hikers and tourists strained to get a closer look. In the excited scramble, no one seemed to notice anything out of the ordinary.

"I wonder...." Blue Bunny was curious. There was something odd about that bear statue.

But Blue Bunny had a suspicion there was more going on here than a quaint photo opportunity.

Blue Bunny backed away from the crowd. They were looking for a secret hiding out, after all. What better place to hide than in plain sight? No one would suspect a malicious bear in a place where you expect to see a well-known helpful bear.

Blue Bunny crept slowly and carefully around the edge of the lodge. Away from the throng, it was quiet. Only the soft whistle of wind met his ears. He found himself on the opposite side of the lodge facing an expanse of glacier topped mountains. Blue Bunny smiled contentedly. He nearly started up his yodeling again when he found himself being lifted by his ears.

A heavy sack dropped over his head. Musty mildew filled his lungs. He tried to twist, to free himself, but the opening of the sack was held tight. It was hard to breathe. Impossible to see. He felt himself being lifted and heaved into a small space. He heard the aching squeak of metal hinges and felt smooth, cool metal against his back.

There was a metal clang, the clink of a key in what sounded like a large lock.

His head felt foggy, his eyelids heavy. Disoriented, everything around him disappeared.

Blue Bunny woke to darkness. He moved his ears, which had just enough room to wiggle in his captive space. They heard a rhythmic clunking, the clanging of machines. Faint whisperings reached his ears. Murmurs of animals.

He caught a piece of conversation. "The boss will be happy. It's the same little long ear bunny. The blue one. Pesky curious little guy he is. Heh, heh, heh. He has the compass. And we have all those maps."

Blue Bunny recognized the voices. They growled just like in the depths of the fort. Cougars.

Suddenly, the sack was lifted from his head. He scrambled to stand, but lost his balance, falling on the hard floor. He blinked at the suddenly bright sun, streaming from widows high above his head.

"You have something the boss wants," growled a gravelly voice. Blue Bunny was face to face with two large cats, one with a trench coat and one with sunglasses. It was the same two feline fiends the bunnies had encountered in the fort. They seem to have successfully escaped the blackberry jam mess. And they were no less focused on getting the compass. Beyond their gleaming teeth, Blue Bunny saw he was in a cavernous room. Pipes and valves and machinery clanked away. The smell of wet wood and rusty metal hung in the air. And the sweet, sticky smell of blackberry.

CHAPTER 12

A SECRET

Brown Bunny looked frantically for his friend. He concluded he must be missing. He needed to find help.

Brown Bunny approached the ranger information station. A brown furry marmot appeared from a small shadowed hole under the desk, flat nose and whiskers wiggling under her broad brimmed hat. She regarded Brown Bunny and whistled, "And you are?"

"Ah, I am Brown Bunny. I'm here to report a suspicious bear sighting."

Dubiously peering at Brown Bunny, she asked, "Can you provide a description of the bear?"

"Well, he was just like any other bear. Claws. Teeth. Fur. All the usual bear things."

"Doesn't sound suspicious to me. Was there anything about him that was not a usual bear thing?"

"Well, now that you mention it, there was a sort of hat. Or belt. Or both. Something like that."

"A hat? Or belt?" Ranger Marmot skeptically questioned.

"Um, I suppose both." Brown Bunny suddenly remembered. "And a shovel. He had a shovel. With a long wood handle. He was mumbling something about fires."

The marmot laughed, "You mean the bear at the entrance? He's a statue!"

"But he winked at my friend. And now my friend's missing."

"Winked? Doubt it. Statues simply do not wink. Just a glint of sun, I suspect," whistled Ranger Marmot definitively. She busied herself with a large pile of papers.

Discouraged, Brown Bunny turned to go. He hesitated at the door. If he didn't find his friend, who would? He turned and chanced one more question, "You have to help me! Not only is my friend missing, but other animals are missing too. And my friend was trying to find them. And if he doesn't find them, who will?"

Ranger Marmot paused, eyes unreadable. She seemed to be considering something. Finally, she tilted her head and walked toward an ordinary looking bookshelf. With a single swift motion, it swung on a hinge, revealing a narrow archway. Ranger Marmot unlocked a single door with a bronze key. She looked back and beckoned Brown Bunny to follow. He was astounded. There was a secret passage inside the lodge?

Meanwhile, Blue Bunny's heart felt like lead. If he gave the cougars the compass, would they let him go? Somehow, he doubted this. Blue Bunny wasn't sure what to do. How had his great adventure come to this? Tears rolled down his furry

face. He reached into his vest pocket in search of a hand-
kerchief, and instead, his paw found something familiar. He
rubbed its smooth surface. The compass had been captured
along with him. He hugged it to his chest, comforted by its
familiar feel. Even without light, he knew its face. His paw
traced its patterns of vines and leaves and blackberries. He
remembered his grandpa's stories. His promise. His chal-
lenge. Blue bunny felt braver.

There must be something he could do. Even if he was
trapped in what appeared to be a dungeon with cougars
for captors.

Above him, a window winked. He heaved himself up
and peeked out. It was night. The silhouettes of weathered
trees danced in moonlight. Blue Bunny strained to see more
of the outside. He saw stars and the faint edge of mountain
peaks. He was still in the lodge! He had often been in its
welcoming walls of wood. It was a place to check maps and
trail conditions. A place of adventure. Of beginnings.

And now he was locked inside it. As far as he could
be from any adventure he willingly chose. He looked up
at the window. The moon hung high and wise. Wisps of
clouds drifted across its face. Perhaps he could climb up to
the window and wriggle free. He contemplated an escape
strategy. Just then he realized he wasn't alone.

Light came from the edges of the doorway and a dark
outline stood in its center. Heart pounding, Blue Bunny
squinted into the darkness. The shape moved closer, swal-
lowing Blue Bunny in its shadow. He shivered.

Blue Bunny stared, equal parts terrified and transfixed.

A deep, throaty voice purred from the corner. The shadow shifted, revealing its great bulk.

A smooth voice emitted from the dark.

"Blue Bunny, Blackberry Keeper—I have been waiting for you."

Blue Bunny held his breath and stepped back. This was no cougar. This was a bear. It stepped forward into the light. Blue Bunny drew breath in.

He had never glimpsed a bear so large. Or so oddly dressed. A gold belt buckle topped a pair of plain blue jeans. A tan hat perched jauntily on his head. This combination was topped by an outlandish trench coat. A statue come to life. Reaching into the coat's depths, the bear revealed row upon row of pockets. From one, he pulled out a shovel.

Blue Bunny winced and closed his eyes. This is it, he thought. This is the end. My life culminates to this.

"Who do you think you are?" snarled the bear.

Blue bunny was silent.

"Who are you?" growled the bear.

Who was he? He was a bunny whose grandpa had taught him and trusted him. He was a bunny who drove mountain roads with his best friend. He was a bunny who braved the inside of a deep, dark fort.

He was a bunny who wanted to do the right thing. He was a bunny who wanted his friends to be free. He was a bunny who wanted the world to not have to hold on so tight, to not be afraid there were not enough good things to share. He was a bunny who wanted to remember the beginning as he was waiting for his end.

Blue Bunny squeezed his eyes shut and waited. Nothing happened. He peeked one eye open. The bear fumbled with the shovel, trying to hold it in one hand and point the other at Blue Bunny.

"Only you can stop hairballs!" the bear bellowed.

Blue Bunny raised an eyebrow.

"No, no, that's not right. Let me try that again," the bear mumbled to himself. He pointed his finger once more. "Only you can combat cats!" the bear cried triumphantly, awaiting Blue Bunny's reaction, which was a look of pure confusion. The bear's grin faded. "No, still not right," he muttered. "Stopping, ceasing, halting...Wait, I remember! Only you can prevent forest flames!" he gleefully yelled.

"Ahhhh, okay," Blue Bunny said, still confused. This bear was oblivious. He flashed a mischievous grin. His teeth gleamed. Was one of them gold? Blue Bunny wondered.

"I am the supreme leader of all pie-dom!" the bear declared, adjusting his hat and flapping the arms of his trench coat.

Blue Bunny stared at him. He tried to remember what Grandpa Bunny would do. "Be still. Listen." he told himself. His ears stood straight up. I hear the end of my current existence.

He was surrounded by the sound of clanging and clunking. Metal and machine. What was this place? Large conveyer belts crisscrossed the expanse of a great room. His eyes adjusted to the dim and followed their haphazard paths. Round tins whizzed by on the belts, spinning and tumbling.

He wasn't in a dungeon. He was in a factory.

CHAPTER 13
BUNNY PIE

The floor was littered with maps. Pocket maps, trail maps. Several globes rolled across the room.

The bear held the largest map, spine cracked, pages brittle. He squinted, turning it upside down and back again. His confusion became frustration. Attempting and failing to fold the unwieldy map, he left it in a crumpled heap.

Blue Bunny's heart sank. The crumpled brittle paper was familiar. He knew its every page. That was his map! From his atlas! With the marking of the tiny blackberry and jagged leaf perched at the top of a mountain. This mountain.

And then he heard a munching sound. Turning toward it, he saw a goat in a black turtleneck, a black beret, and large horn-rimmed glasses, eating a discarded map. "Hey, cool cat," called a familiar, but discouraged voice.

"Beat Nick! What are you doing here?" exclaimed Blue Bunny.

Beat shrugged his shoulders and pointed to his hooves, which were surrounded by shackles. "Don't have a choice, do I?" he asked, sounding disheartened. "As soon as you and your friend left the co-op, a couple of cougars showed up and drug me here. Not cool, cats. Not cool. They made all these folks come here too."

Blue Bunny looked deeper into the dark. Dozens of animals, chained and weary, looked back at him. His eyes met a pair of familiar ones, sad and resigned. He gasped. Margaret! And Roy Beaver!

"They made me give them all my berries," Roy lamented.

Blue Bunny peered further into the shadows. Myrtle the baker! "The cougars wanted my pie recipe," she cried.

Blue Bunny suddenly realized. Of course. This is where the animals had vanished. This is where the blackberries had vanished. This is where the atlas had vanished. The atlas, his precious books of maps, had been here all along. But the bear clearly didn't understand the map. Without the compass, he didn't understand how to read it, how to follow it. Blue Bunny longed to pick up the squashed map, to smooth its pages and hold its magic close.

He was startled by a growl. "You, Blue Bunny, will give me the compass. You will lead me to the blackberries." The bear was growing louder, more animated. "With those blackberries I will make pie. Pie! Pie!"

"But I don't think I can do that," said Blue Bunny in a small voice, thinking about bear's enormous teeth. The bear laughed, a giggle, so discordant with his demeanor. He quickly suppressed the giggle into a deep chuckle, "Heh, heh, heh."

The bear grew more animated, "I will have pie! Pie! The greatest pie empire any animal has ever known!" What started as a maniacal laugh oscillated to a dreamy giggle. "Tee-hee."

What was going on? Blue Bunny studied the bear. The gigantic trench coat. The odd hat. The glinting teeth. The bear smiled, and as he did, the gold tooth popped off.

The bear clapped a paw over his mouth and hurriedly pulled an eye patch from one voluminous pocket. He placed it on his left eye, squinting at Blue Bunny. He switched to his right eye and squinted even more. Blue Bunny simply stared. "Too much?" the bear inquired, slumping his shoulders.

The bear was trying to be villainous. And he wasn't doing a very good job. Up close, he seemed somehow lonely and uncertain.

But he had to be villainous, Blue Bunny told himself. He stole the atlas. He kidnapped animals. He forced them to work. And now he was demanding Blue Bunny give him the precious compass, just so he could hoard the blackberries and eat all the pie he wanted. He was the bad guy in this story.

But what if Blue Bunny did give the bear the compass? As a trade. What if this was the way to rescue his friends? Would the bear let them go once he had both the map and the compass and could find the blackberries all on his own?

Blue Bunny reached into his vest pocket. He felt for his familiar compass, and was reassured by its smooth surface. Just as he was about to remove it from his pocket and hand it over, he felt the ground beneath him move.

Blue Bunny nearly fell. He regained his balance just in time to be whisked across the room, straight toward a wall.

Shutting his eyes and bracing for impact, his body turned, then turned again. Blue Bunny was on a conveyer belt. He looked behind him to see the bear waving farewell. "This is your fate unless you hand over the compass," the bear called.

Blue Bunny sped under a huge arched sign, "Bear's Pie-O-Matic". He was riding a blackberry pie making machine. Shiny metal arms slammed in rhythm. Gears and pipes rattled. Ahead of him, pie tins clattered along the conveyer belt. They paused beneath a series of nozzles, gaping mouths oozing purple gelatinous goo and sticky dough. The belt jolted, whirling the tins and Blue Bunny forward. He watched in fascinated horror as the tins traveled under a knife, which cut the dough quickly and wildly, leaving behind perfectly round pie. Just beyond, yawned an oven.

Blue Bunny was almost directly beneath the goo nozzle. Pie filling spat out in rhythm. The glinting knife and hungry oven lay not far beyond. Three pies were ahead of him. He had a few more seconds. Blue Bunny scrambled backward on the belt. He did not intend to become bunny pie.

CHAPTER 14

RESCUE

Brown Bunny hesitated at the entrance of the secret passage. His heart was pounding. He knew what needed to be done. His best friend needed rescuing and he was the one to do it. Before sneaking into depths unknown, he needed a plan. He needed a disguise. A delicious disguise. He needed supplies. And supplies were contained in the truck.

An inventory of its contents revealed 27 jam packets, a partial roll of duct tape, a ripped boat sail, various sailing lines, scraps of wood, and a small camping hatchet. Brown Bunny surveyed this odd assortment. What sort of disguise could he create from this quirky collection?

What would tempt an animal looking for a secret blackberry grove? An animal who had the map to the blackberries but couldn't read it?

Blackberry pie, of course.

He set to work. Soon, he had created a large round frame of rope and wood. He stretched the boat sail across its expanse. Straining against the taunt fabric, he fastened everything together with copious amounts of duct tape, careful to leave tiny holes for his ears and paws. From there, he slathered jam across its boat sail crust.

He stood back. In front of him lay the largest blackberry pie he had ever seen. He climbed inside it.

Crouched inside his creation, Brown Bunny threaded his ears through two slits at its top. Satisfied with his plan, he crept into the secret passage, painstakingly inching the enormous pie along with him. He was odd sight, a giant walking pie with bunny ears.

He could hear his own shuffling and breathing inside the giant pie. And he heard a humming. It grew louder and became a clanging.

He stopped abruptly at the sound of distant footsteps. As they faded, Brown Bunny moved forward once again.

Finally, he reached a door. "Knock, knock. Special delivery." Brown Bunny held his breath. He sure hoped this would work. He called out again.

The bear turned away from Blue Bunny toward the entrance to the factory. "Now who could that be?" he wondered aloud. The bear sauntered to the door. "Who is it?" he growled.

"Mrrph mrung muff. Eh hum, I mean, I have a special delivery for a Mr. Bear," came a muffled voice through the door.

"How do I know I can trust you?" the bear replied.

"This is a very, very special delivery, for only the most marvelous, revered of bears."

The bear grinned, puffed his chest and adjusted his hat.

Tempted by his own self-proclaimed importance, he flung open the door.

"Yes?" he cooed, eyes gleaming. "I, most marvelous and revered of bears, am ready." He looked around for his special surprise and spotted the largest pie he had ever seen.

Entranced, he leaned down. The tantalizing smell of blackberries wafted into his nostrils. Drool dripped from his teeth.

He lifted the pie from the ground. Inside, Brown Bunny trembled. He needed to think very quickly and jump very swiftly before he found his way into this bear's mouth.

The bear hummed in anticipation. "Valderi, valdera, Valderi, valdera-ha-ha-ha-ha-ha." A gleeful giggle escaped his throat. Grinning, he brought the enormous pie to his lips. He bit down, anticipating the tang of blackberries. The crust gave way to air. It was empty.

"What?" the bear growled, confused and enraged. "What kind of pie is this?"

"A tricky one," exclaimed Brown Bunny, bounding out and away from the bottom of the pie, through a cleverly installed escape hatch. "Where are you, Blue Bunny?"

"Here, here I am," yelped his relieved friend, who was scrambling atop the moving conveyer belt. "You found me!"

Brown Bunny ran to his friend. "Quick, this way!" he cried. Blue Bunny tried to leap from the conveyer belt, but couldn't. Desperate to keep his paws beneath him, he clamored for the edge. The slick metal evaded his grip and sent him spinning.

The bear lunged after him. "I'll get you!" he roared.

"What do you want, bear?" gasped Blue Bunny, his heart and paws trying to keep pace with his tumbling body.

Blue Bunny called out again. "Why did you think you could have all the blackberries for yourself?"

The bear stumbled against the machinery, knocking against a large red button that slowed and stopped the belt. "The blackberries are so delicious," he moaned. "And there aren't enough to share. If I give away the blackberries, there won't be any left for me. For the bears. We deserve all the blackberries."

Blue Bunny certainly did not want to share the blackberries with the bear. The bear didn't deserve them, after all. Wasn't he the one who kidnapped all the animals, tried to keep all the pie for himself, and was currently holding him prisoner?

No. Blue Bunny did not want to share with the bear. And he no longer wanted to be the Blackberry Keeper it if meant spending one more second with this horrible creature. Silencing his heart, Blue Bunny leapt from the finally quiet pie making machine and prepared to be rid of this bad guy, once and for all.

And then Big Bear started crying. Hot tears ran down his face. They dripped from his fur onto his coat and splattered on the floor. Startled, Blue Bunny watched Big Bear slump to the floor. "Go," he said. "Go away from here. All of you. Cougars, release the prisoners. I can't do anything right. I can't read the map. I can't find the blackberries. I can't make pie. I can't even be a good villain."

He wrenched off the trench coat, pulled frantically at the

eye patch, and clawed at the enormous hat. Everything scary about Big Bear fell to the floor. At the loss of his costume, he began to cry all the more. Great sobs came from his chest.

As Blue Bunny watched Big Bear remove his disguise, layer by layer, Blue Bunny realized he was crying too.

Blue Bunny's heart got very quiet. He listened. He heard the whisper of the map. He heard Wise Raven's promise. He heard his longing to be part of something bigger. And he wondered if Big Bear wanted to be part of that something too.

Blue Bunny had a feeling the truth was about to reveal itself. And it was bigger than he ever understood it to be.

Maybe there was more to being the Blackberry Keeper than keeping blackberries. Maybe Blue Bunny needed to share them. Maybe he was just as afraid of scarcity as Big Bear. Maybe he needed to let go. Maybe this was his something that was hard. That was scary. That was uncertain.

Should he give Big Bear a chance?

As soon as he asked the question, he felt something loosen in his chest. Blue Bunny spotted the map, abandoned on the floor. As he looked at it, more and more blackberries appeared. They spread and bloomed and grew as he watched, jagged leaves and intricate vines unfurling across the paper, blanketing it in a lush layer of abundance, until everything else on the map become nearly invisible.

Blue Bunny had never seen the map this way before. He was disoriented and astonished. But I thought the blackberries were rare, he thought. I thought I was supposed to keep them hidden and protected.

A tiny voice whispered from the map, "You only believed they were rare."

And then Blue Bunny remembered. He remembered his invitation to the story. He remembered his invitation to abundance. And the deepest part of his heart, the part he could hear only if he was very quiet, for the first time felt full.

He turned to Big Bear.

"How would you like to come to a feast?"

Big Bear turned, surprised. "A feast? I've never been invited to a feast. After I tried to take all the blackberries, who would want me there?"

"I want you there," replied Blue Bunny.

CHAPTER 15

FREEDOM

Big Bear was seated at an expansive table. Plates and platters of blackberries covered its surface. He felt a brand-new feeling. A feeling of contentment. Eyes shining and mouth watering, he anticipated the feast. Blue Bunny set an enormous slice of pie, dripping with luscious dark berries, before him. Big Bear took a bite. He felt another brand-new feeling. Joy.

As Blue Bunny watched, he knew. He knew this was what being the Blackberry Keeper was all about. He turned to his friend, his friend that had helped do the right thing even when it was hard.

"I think we need a new name," said Blue Bunny. "Keeping the blackberries isn't nearly as wonderful as giving them away."

"Agreed. And we need a new outfit," replied Brown Bunny, grinning. "This is what the Blackberry Keeper is meant to wear," he said, beckoning Blue Bunny to lean forward. He slipped an apron over his friend's ears and pointed to the letters printed across the front: "Blackberry Server".

Blue Bunny laughed. He laughed with relief his friends were safe. He laughed with joy at the table set before him. He laughed with the freedom of letting go.

His laugh was echoed by music. Blue Bunny searched for its source and was surprised to discover the cougars playing a perky polka. They had traded trench coats and sunglasses for elaborately embroidered lederhosen and formed an oom-pah band, conducted by none other than a beaming Roy Beaver. One cougar was vigorously blowing air through a tuba and the other was clawing an accordion. What they lacked in skill, they made up in enthusiasm.

Grandpa Bunny happily hummed along, pausing occasionally to sip through a straw. "This is the best blackberry milkshake I have ever had," he pronounced.

Blue Bunny spotted Beat Nick munching on a fresh vine, thorns and all. Myrtle and Margaret giggled over a pot of jam. Bunnies and chipmunks and deer gathered at immense tables, enjoying sweet shared treats of blackberry milkshakes, blackberry ice cream, blackberry jam, black-berry candy, and of course, blackberry pie.

No matter how many pies they served, there were always more. They never ran out. Drippy, sticky blackberries over-flowed, staining mouths deep purple.

It was better than Blue Bunny imagined. Better than he thought possible. It was the story his heart knew. The one he was created for. It was the story of enough. He took a satisfying bite of pie.

EPILOGUE

Out of the corner of his eye, Blue Bunny saw a sheen of black. Curious, he turned and saw a magnificent bird with feathers so dark, they reflected rainbows.

She tilted her head, dark and regal, her piercing gaze simultaneously capturing him and setting him free. Blue Bunny stared at her and she stared back, her eyes two ebony mirrors. In them, he saw himself. He felt if he looked long enough, stared hard enough, he may find all the answers.

Blue Bunny wondered if she had been there the whole time. He wondered if, through all the wandering, through all the uncertainty, she was there, before him and behind him and beside him.

He wondered if all his listening—to the story, to Grandpa, to the map, to his heart—was all just listening to her.

Wise Raven held his gaze for one more lingering moment. Then she winked and flew to the mountaintop.

Made in the USA
Middletown, DE
03 September 2020